EARTH WEATHER

AS EXPLAINED BY

Professor Xargle

Library of Congress Cataloging-in-Publication Data
Willis, Jeanne. [Dr. Xargle's book of earth weather]
Earth weather as explained by Professor Xargle /
translated into human by Jeanne Willis; illustrated by
Tony Ross.—1st American ed.   p.   cm.   Originally published:
Dr. Xargle's book of earth weather. London: Andersen Press, 1991.
Summary: Professor Xargle explains to his class of extraterrestrials
how humans behave in different kinds of weather.   ISBN 0-525-45025-4
[1. Weather—Fiction.   2. Extraterrestrials—Fiction.
3. Humorous stories.]   I. Ross, Tony, ill.   II. Title.
PZ7.W68313Eaqb   1993   [E]—dc20
92-14067   CIP   AC

First published in the United States 1993 by
Dutton Children's Books,
a division of Penguin Books USA Inc.
375 Hudson Street, New York, New York 10014
Originally published in Great Britain 1991 by
Andersen Press Ltd., London
Printed in Italy by Grafiche AZ, Verona
First American Edition
1   3   5   7   9   10   8   6   4   2

EARTH WEATHER

AS EXPLAINED BY

Professor Xargle

Translated into Human by **JEANNE WILLIS**
Illustrated by **TONY ROSS**

DUTTON CHILDREN'S BOOKS ★ NEW YORK

Good morning, class.

Today we are going to learn about the weather on Planet Earth.

There are four kinds.
Too hot, too cold, too wet, and too windy.

Unlike us, Earthlets are not waterproof. In the rain-goop, they wear a loose plastic skin so that they do not get soggy.

Some Earthlets grow large rubber feet that will not come off.

To keep water off their one small brain, Earthlets carry
a head protector with sharp points. Sometimes the
head protectors get bored and attack the Earthlet.

Other Earthlets use their protectors to collect extra pairs of eyegoggles.

Earthlets who have nothing better to do go out in the hot and lie in nests of brown sugar. They wear only their underfrillies and rub each other with butterglob.

Then they stretch out in the shape of a star. When they turn brown, it means they are cooked.

But never eat them.

Sometimes an Earthlet gets overcooked. To cure him, walk up and slap him hard on the back.

Other Earthlings do not like the hot. They roll up their legskins and stand in a giant bathtub with nostril wipers on their heads.

On breezy days, here are some things to avoid:

flying pretend hairdos,

billowing outergarments of female Earthlings,

pink-knitted sugar that has escaped from its stick.

When it turns cold, Planet Earth is invaded by strange white visitors with black eyes and orange noses.

They hold brooms but refuse to sweep up. They stand still all day, smoking their pipes.

Small Earthlets find it difficult to stand on the white stuff. Their parents must drag them here and there on blocks of wood.

Warlike Earthlets make round missiles out of white stuff and throw them at furry strangers.

To protect themselves from cold, Earthlets wear bag-lets on the end of their tentacles. They also put on a padded bubble called an orak and pump it up with air.

If the headpiece is not tied on tightly under the gargle, other Earthlets may sneak up and stuff it full of ice missiles.

That is the end of today's lesson. Put on your disguises and gather your carol sheets.

We are going to sing on the doorsteps of Earthlings.
Apparently it is their custom to do this in the month
of July.

All together now: *"Hark the horrid angels sing . . ."*